Peace Paz Paix Pace Frieden Mir Rauha Vrede Fred Sidi
Vrede Beke Pokoj Paco Pax Bariş A... Salam
Aman Hau Mier Amani Fifa Jam Frieden Erkigsinek Pasch
Sula Sulh Paci Damai Shalom Shanti Peace Paz Paix Pace
Frieden Mir Rauha Vrede Fred Sidi Vrede Beke Pokoj Paco
Pax Bariş Asomdwoe Pake Salam Aman Hau Mier Amani
Fifa Jam Frieden Erkigsinek Pasch Sula Sulh Paci Damai
Shalom Shanti Peace Paz Paix Pace Frieden Mir Rauha
Vrede Fred Sidi Vrede Beke Pokoj Paco Pax Bariş
Asomdwoe Pake Salam Aman Hau Mier Amani Fifa Jam
Frieden Erkigsinek Pasch Sula Sulh Paci Damai Shalom
Shanti Peace Paz Paix Pace Frieden Mir Rauha Vrede
Fred Sidi Vrede Beke Pokoj Paco Pax Bariş Asomdwoe Pake
Salam Aman Hau Mier Amani Fifa Jam Frieden Erkigsinek
Pasch Sula Sulh Paci Damai Shalom Shanti Peace Paz Paix
Pace Frieden Mir Rauha Vrede Fred Sidi Vrede Beke Pokoj
Paco Pax Bariş Asomdwoe Pake Salam Aman Hau Mier
Amani Fifa Jam Frieden Erkigsinek Pasch Sula Sulh Paci
Damai Shalom Shanti Peace Paz Paix Pace Frieden Mir
Rauha Vrede Fred Sidi Vrede Beke Pokoj Paco Pax Bariş
Asomdwoe Pake Salam Aman Hau Mier Amani Fifa Jam
Frieden Erkigsinek Pasch Sula Sulh Paci Damai Shalom
Shanti Peace Paz Paix Pace Frieden Mir Rauha Vrede
Fred Sidi Vrede Beke Pokoj Paco Pax Bariş Asomdwoe Pake
Salam Aman Hau Mier Amani Fifa Jam Frieden Erkigsinek
Pasch Sula Sulh Paci Damai Shalom Shanti Peace Paz Paix
Pace Frieden Mir Rauha Vrede Fred Sidi Vrede Beke Pokoj

Peace Paz Paix Pace Frieden Mir Rauha Vrede Fred Sidi
Vrede Beke Pokoj Paco Pax Bariş Asomdwoe Pake Salam
Aman Hau Mier Amani Fifă Jam Frieden Erkigsinek Pasch
Sula Sulh Paci Damai Shalom Shanti Peace Paz Paix Pace
Frieden Mir Rauha Vrede Fred Sidi Vrede Beke Pokoj Paco
Pax Bariş Asomdwoe Pake Salam Aman Hau Mier Aman
Fifă Jam Frieden Erkigsinek Pasch Sula Sulh Paci Dama
Shalom Shanti Peace Paz Paix Pace Frieden Mir Rauha
Vrede Fred Sidi Vrede Beke Pokoj Paco Pax Bariş
Asomdwoe Pake Salam Aman Hau Mier Amani Fifă Jam
Frieden Erkigsinek Pasch Sula Sulh Paci Damai Shalom
Shanti Peace Paz Paix Pace Frieden Mir Rauha Vrede
Fred Sidi Vrede Beke Pokoj Paco Pax Bariş Asomdwoe Pake
Salam Aman Hau Mier Amani Fifă Jam Frieden Erkigsinek
Pasch Sula Sulh Paci Damai Shalom Shanti Peace Paz Paix
Pace Frieden Mir Rauha Vrede Fred Sidi Vrede Beke Pokoj
Paco Pax Bariş Asomdwoe Pake Salam Aman Hau Mier
Amani Fifă Jam Frieden Erkigsinek Pasch Sula Sulh Paci
Damai Shalom Shanti Peace Paz Paix Pace Frieden Mir
Rauha Vrede Fred Sidi Vrede Beke Pokoj Paco Pax Bariş
Asomdwoe Pake Salam Aman Hau Mier Amani Fifă Jam
Frieden Erkigsinek Pasch Sula Sulh Paci Damai Shalom
Shanti Peace Paz Paix Pace Frieden Mir Rauha Vrede
Fred Sidi Vrede Beke Pokoj Paco Pax Bariş Asomdwoe Pake
Salam Aman Hau Mier Amani Fifă Jam Frieden Erkigsinek
Pasch Sula Sulh Paci Damai Shalom Shanti Peace Paz Paix
Pace Frieden Mir Rauha Vrede Fred Sidi Vrede Beke Poko

LET THERE BE LIGHT

Let There Be Light

POEMS AND PRAYERS FOR REPAIRING THE WORLD

Compiled and illustrated by
JANE BRESKIN ZALBEN

DUTTON CHILDREN'S BOOKS
NEW YORK

I wish to thank the following people for being there: Stephanie Owens Lurie, Marilyn E. Marlow, Dr. Ellyn Altman, Eve Feldman, Dr. Nancy Braman, Cathy Schrier, Betsy Silverstein, Helen and Richie Albertson, Cathy Graham, Mae Breskin, Dr. Stephen Breskin, Steven Zalben (once again), and Zoë Zalben for cuddling when I needed it. I would also like to add my appreciation to the librarians at the Port Washington Library Reference and Children's Rooms for culling through information sources with me.

ACKNOWLEDGMENTS

p. 11: Eastern Eskimo prayer from *Songs of the Dream People: Chants and Images from the Indians and Eskimos of North America*, edited and illustrated by James Houston (Atheneum, New York), copyright © 1972 by James Houston.

pp. 14-15: Passages from the Koran, translated by N.J. Dawood (Penguin Classics, 1956; fifth revised edition 1990), copyright © N.J. Dawood, 1956, 1959, 1966, 1968, 1974, 1990.

p. 17: Native American prayer from *Earth Always Endures: Native American Poems*, edited by Neil Philip, (Viking/Penguin Putnam, 1996).

p. 26: From *An Open Heart*, by The Dalai Lama, copyright © 2001 by His Holiness The Dalai Lama. By permission of Little, Brown and Company (Inc.).

p. 29: Passages from "Desiderata" by Max Ehrmann, copyright © 1927 by Max Ehrmann. All rights reserved. Reprinted by permission Robert L. Bell, Melrose, Mass. 02176 USA.

CIP Data is available.

Published in the United States 2002 by Dutton Children's Books,
a division of Penguin Putnam Books for Young Readers
345 Hudson Street, New York, New York 10014
www.penguinputnam.com
Designed by Gloria Cheng
Printed in Hong Kong • First Edition
ISBN 0-525-46995-8
10 9 8 7 6 5 4 3 2 1

For Alexander and Jonathan

I pray our family continues to grow through love,
and, with it, the world.

Dear God,
Be good to me.
The sea is so wide,
And my boat is so small.

PRAYER OF A BRETON FISHERMAN

According to a sixteenth-century *midrash* (a legend based on a biblical text) by Rabbi Isaac Luria, when God made the world He planned to put sparks of light into everything. The holy light was stored in vessels, but it was so strong that the vessels broke into millions of pieces. People were created to find the shards and bring them together to restore the vessels, thereby "repairing the world" (*tikkun olam* in Hebrew). Dr. Rachel Naomi Remen writes in her book *My Grandfather's Blessings* that we restore the holiness of creation through our loving kindness and compassion, and every act, no matter how big or small, repairs the world. "We are all here…to grow in wisdom and to learn to love better."

The concept of healing the world is common to many religions—a fact that was confirmed for me when I researched the text selections for this book. I deliberately chose poems, prayers, and quotes from a variety of faiths and cultures that would express complementary ideas, such as the importance of friendship, love, and small, fleeting moments. My aim was to make a book that would wrap readers in comfort like a warm quilt as it helped them understand and appreciate each other's similarities and differences.

I wanted the illustrations for this book to be as varied as the text selections, and so I employed styles, techniques, materials, and patterns from different cultures. The artwork—a combination of cut paper, digital manipulation, collage, and painting—incorporates Japanese rice paper from the 1930s; papyrus from the Nile River in Cairo; paper made from the bark of African and Middle Eastern trees; and paper from Nepal, India, and Italy. I took inspiration from Persian miniatures, illuminated manuscripts, Islamic tiles, and works by Matisse and abstract expressionists. I enjoyed the creative challenge of interpreting each selection in a different way.

In closing, I would like to quote the Dalai Lama, who said in a speech to thousands gathered in New York City's Central Park in the summer of 1999: "Whether you are religious or not, we all wish for happiness. As long as we are part of human society, it is very important to be a kind, warm-hearted person." May our hearts join in friendship and understanding as we all do our part to repair the world.

JANE BRESKIN ZALBEN

In the Beginning God created the heaven and the earth.
And the earth was waste and void; and darkness was upon
    the face of the deep.
And the spirit of God moved upon the face of the waters.
And God said, Let there be light: and there was light.
And God saw the light, that it was good: and God divided
    the light from the darkness.
And God called the light Day, and the darkness he called Night.
And there was evening and there was morning, the first day.

GENESIS

"The heavens are the heavens of the Lord"—
they are already heavenly in character.
"But the earth He has given to mortals"—
so that we might make of it something heavenly.

Light and darkness, night and day.
We marvel at the mystery of stars.
Moon and sky, sand and sea.
We marvel at the mystery of sun.
Twilight, high noon, dusk, and dawn.
Though we are mortal, we are Creation's crown.
Flesh and bone, steel and stone.
We dwell in fragile, temporary shelters.
Grant steadfast love, compassion, and grace.
Sustain us, Lord; our origin is dust.
Splendor, mercy, majesty, love endure.
We are but little lower than the angels.
Resplendent skies, sunset, sunrise.
The grandeur of Creation lifts our lives.
Evening darkness, morning dawn.
Renew our lives as You renew all time.

THE FIRST *BERAKHAH* (PRAYER),
GIFT OF CREATION,
BEFORE K'RIAT SH'MA
SIDDUR, SHABBAT EVENING SERVICE

I arise with movements
Swift as a raven's wing,
I arise to meet the day.
My face is turned from the dark of night
To gaze at the new dawn whitening the sky.

EASTERN ESKIMO PRAYER

In dwelling, live close to the ground.
In thinking, keep to the simple.
In conflict, be fair and generous.
In governing, don't try to control.
In work, do what you enjoy.
In family life, be completely present.

LAO-TZU
6TH CENTURY B.C.E.
TAO TE CHING

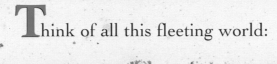

Think of all this fleeting world:

A star at dawn, a bubble in a stream;
A flash of lightning in a summer cloud,
A flickering lamp, a phantom, and a dream.

THE BUDDHA
6TH CENTURY B.C.E.

A good word is as a good tree—
its roots are firm,
and its branches are in the sky;
it gives fruit every season
by the leave of its Lord.

QUR'AN (The Koran) *14:24–27*

In the name of God, the Compassionate, the Merciful

my Lord, inspire me
That I may be thankful for Your blessing.
Wherewith You have blessed me and my father and mother,
And that I may do good works that please You.

QUR'AN (The Koran) *46:15*

Lift the stone and you will find me;
Cleave the wood and I am there.

THE SAYINGS OF JESUS

Let me learn the lessons
You have hidden in every leaf and rock.

NATIVE AMERICAN PRAYER

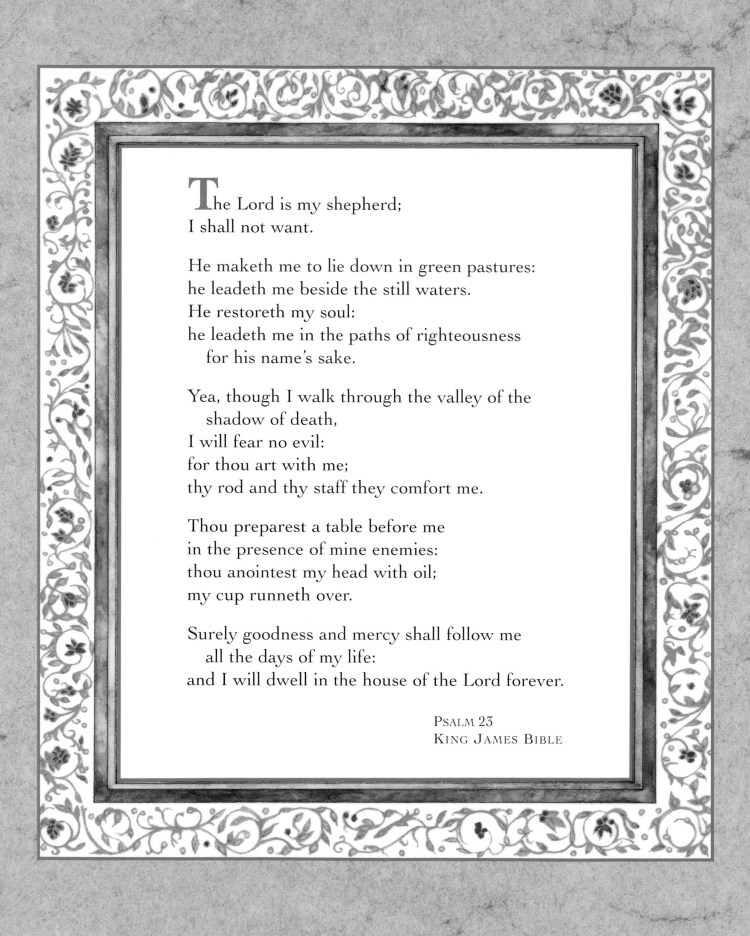

The Lord is my shepherd;
I shall not want.

He maketh me to lie down in green pastures:
he leadeth me beside the still waters.
He restoreth my soul:
he leadeth me in the paths of righteousness
   for his name's sake.

Yea, though I walk through the valley of the
   shadow of death,
I will fear no evil:
for thou art with me;
thy rod and thy staff they comfort me.

Thou preparest a table before me
in the presence of mine enemies:
thou anointest my head with oil;
my cup runneth over.

Surely goodness and mercy shall follow me
   all the days of my life:
and I will dwell in the house of the Lord forever.

PSALM 23
KING JAMES BIBLE

Lord, make me an instrument of thy peace;
Where there is hatred, let me sow love;
Where there is injury, pardon;
Where there is discord, union;
Where there is doubt, faith;
Where there is despair, hope;
Where there is darkness, light;
Where there is sadness, joy.

St. Francis of Assisi, 13th century

To every thing there is a season,
And a time to every purpose under the heaven:
There is a time for all things under the sun:
A time to be born and a time to die;
A time to plant and a time to pluck;
A time to kill and a time to heal;
A time to break down and a time to build up;
A time to weep and a time to laugh;
A time to mourn and a time to dance;
A time to cast away stones, and a time to gather;
A time to embrace and a time to refrain;
A time to seek and a time to lose;
A time to keep and a time to cast away,
A time to rend and a time to sew,
A time to keep silence and a time to speak,
A time to love and a time to hate,
A time to forget and a time to remember.
A time of war and a time of peace.

ECCLESIASTES 3:1–9

Who sews the heavens like cloth:
May you knit together that which is below.

SHONA PRAYER (ZIMBABWE)
AFRICAN TRADITIONAL RELIGION

Let us be at peace,
Let the souls of the people be cool.

NUER PRAYER (SUDAN)
AFRICAN TRADITIONAL RELIGION

May the poor find wealth,
Those weak with sorrow find joy.
May the forlorn find new hope,
Constant happiness and prosperity.

May the frightened cease to be afraid,
And those bound be free.
May the weak find power,
And may their hearts join in friendship.

HIS HOLINESS, THE DALAI LAMA

Go placidly amid the noise and the haste,
and remember what peace there may be in silence.
You are a child of the universe, no less than the trees and the stars;
  you have a right to be here. And whether or not it is clear to you,
  no doubt the universe is unfolding as it should.
Therefore be at peace with God,
  whatever you conceive Him to be.
And whatever your labors and aspirations,
  in the noisy confusion of life, keep peace in your soul.
With all its sham, drudgery, and broken dreams,
  it is still a beautiful world.
Be cheerful. Strive to be happy.

FROM "DESIDERATA," BY MAX EHRMANN

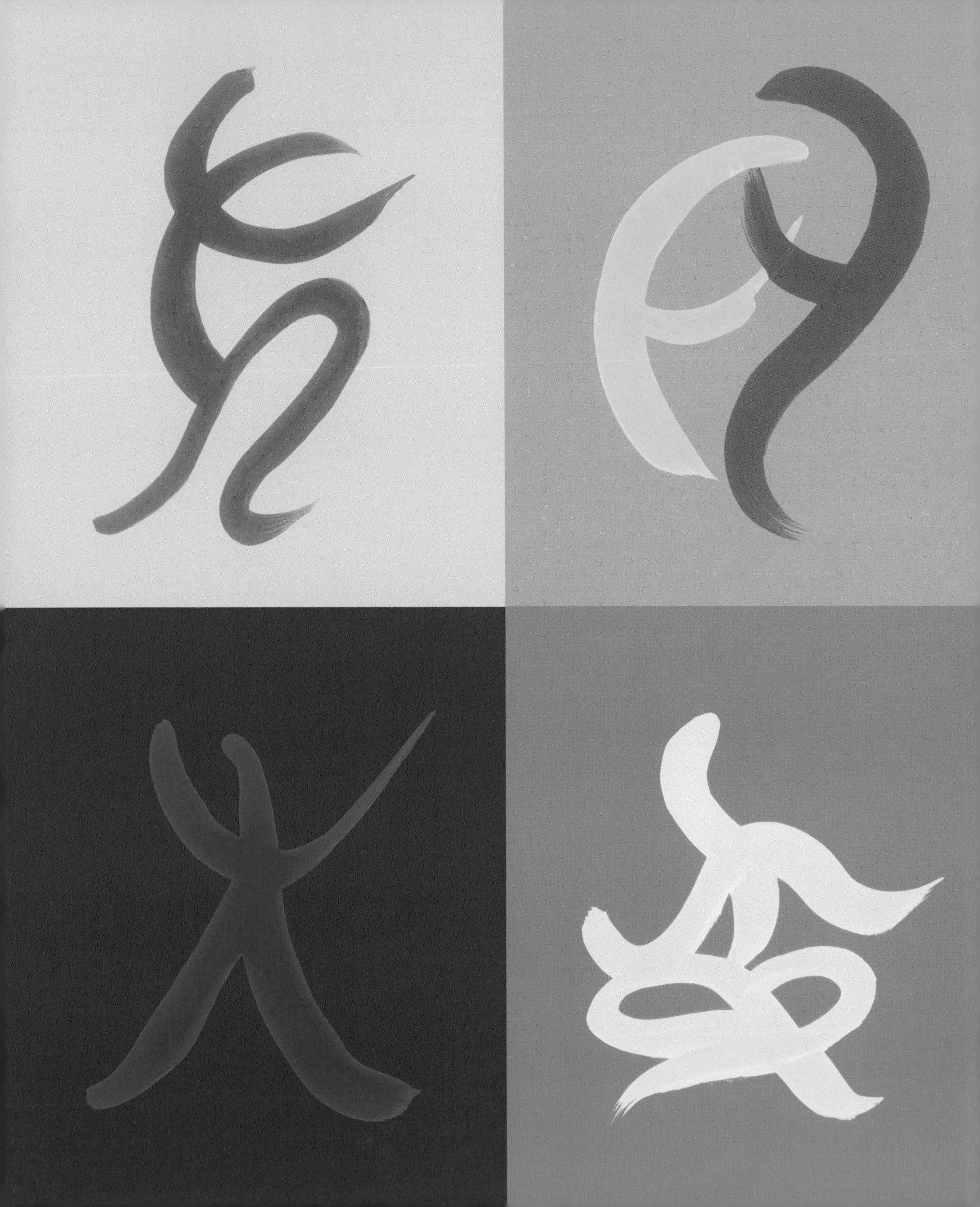

dance

as though no one is watching you,

love

as though you have never been hurt before,

sing

as though no one can hear you,

live

as though heaven is on earth.

AUTHOR UNKNOWN

Love is the strongest force the world possesses,
and yet it is the humblest imaginable.

MAHATMA GANDHI

Peace Paz Paix Pace Frieden Mir Rauha Vrede Fred Sidi
Vrede Beke Pokoj Paco Pax Barış Asomdwoe Pake Salam
Aman Hau Mier Amani Sifa Jam Frieden Erkigsineh Pasch
Sula Sulh Paci Damai Shalom Shanti Peace Paz Paix Pace
Frieden Mir Rauha Vrede Fred Sidi Vrede Beke Pokoj Paco
Pax Barış Asomdwoe Pake Salam Aman Hau Mier Amani
Sifa Jam Frieden Erkigsineh Pasch Sula Sulh Paci Damai
Shalom Shanti Peace Paz Paix Pace Frieden Mir Rauha
Vrede Fred Sidi Vrede Beke Pokoj Paco Pax Barış
Asomdwoe Pake Salam Aman Hau Mier Amani Sifa Jam
Frieden Erkigsineh Pasch Sula Sulh Paci Damai Shalom
Shanti Peace Paz Paix Pace Frieden Mir Rauha Vrede
Fred Sidi Vrede Beke Pokoj Paco Pax Barış Asomdwoe Pake
Salam Aman Hau Mier Amani Sifa Jam Frieden Erkigsineh
Pasch Sula Sulh Paci Damai Shalom Shanti Peace Paz Paix
Pace Frieden Mir Rauha Vrede Fred Sidi Vrede Beke Pokoj
Paco Pax Barış Asomdwoe Pake Salam Aman Hau Mier
Amani Sifa Jam Frieden Erkigsineh Pasch Sula Sulh Paci
Damai Shalom Shanti Peace Paz Paix Pace Frieden Mir
Rauha Vrede Fred Sidi Vrede Beke Pokoj Paco Pax Barış
Asomdwoe Pake Salam Aman Hau Mier Amani Sifa Jam
Frieden Erkigsineh Pasch Sula Sulh Paci Damai Shalom
Shanti Peace Paz Paix Pace Frieden Mir Rauha Vrede
Fred Sidi Vrede Beke Pokoj Paco Pax Barış Asomdwoe Pake
Salam Aman Hau Mier Amani Sifa Jam Frieden Erkigsineh
Pasch Sula Sulh Paci Damai Shalom Shanti Peace Paz Paix
Pace Frieden Mir Rauha Vrede Fred Sidi Vrede Beke Pokoj